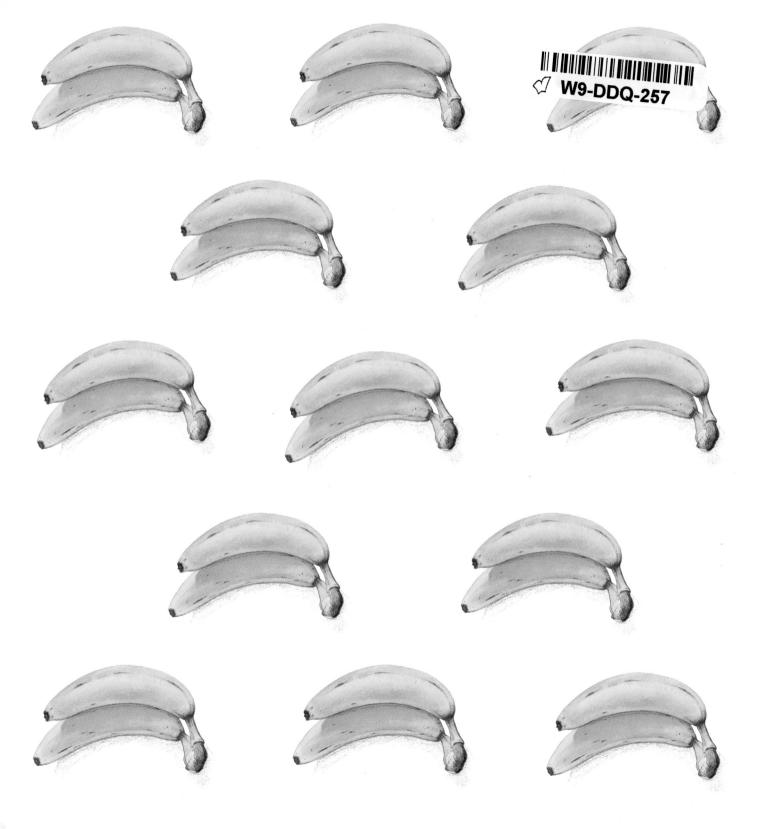

Douglas & McIntyre Ltd.
585 Bloor Street West
Toronto, Canada M6G 1K5

Canadian Cataloguing in Publication Data
Browne, Anthony
Willy and Hugh
ISBN 0-88894-843-3
I. Title.
PZ7.B766Wi 1991   j823′.914   C90-095748-4

Printed and bound in Belgium by
Proost International Book Production

Anthony Browne

WILLY AND HUGH

Douglas & McIntyre
Vancouver/Toronto

Willy was lonely.

Everyone seemed to have friends.

Everyone except Willy.

No-one let him join in any games;
they all said he was useless.

One day Willy was
walking in the park ...

minding his own business ...

 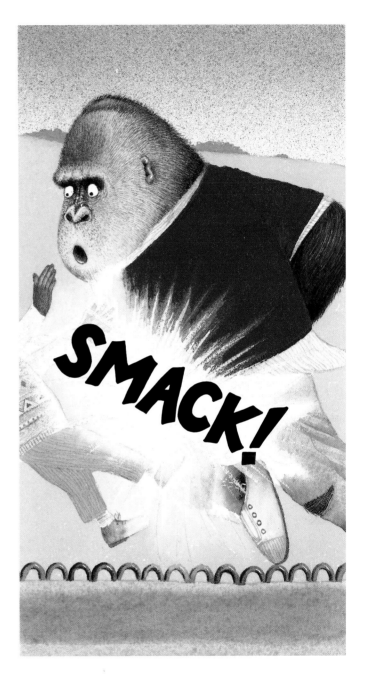

and Hugh Jape was running ...   they met.

"Oh, I'm so sorry," said Hugh.

Willy was amazed. "But *I'm* sorry," he said, "I wasn't watching where I was going."

"No, it was *my* fault," said Hugh. "I wasn't looking where *I* was going. I'm sorry."

Hugh helped Willy to his feet.

They sat down on a bench
and watched the joggers.
"Looks like they're *really*
enjoying themselves,"
said Hugh.
Willy laughed.

Buster Nose appeared. "I've been looking for you, little wimp," he sneered.

Hugh stood up. "Can *I* be of any help?" he asked.
Buster left. Very quickly.

So Willy and Hugh decided to go to the zoo.

Then they went
to the library, and
Willy read to Hugh.

As they were leaving the library,
Hugh stopped suddenly...

He'd seen a TERRIFYING CREATURE...

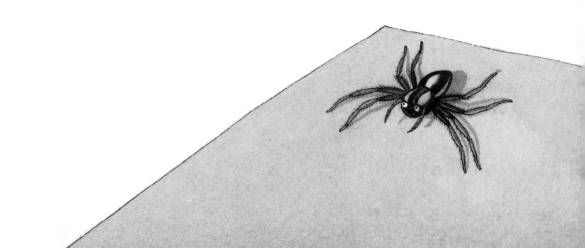

"Can *I* be of any help?" asked Willy, and he carefully moved the spider out of the way.

Willy felt quite pleased with himself.

"Shall we meet up tomorrow?" asked Hugh.

"Yes, that would be great," said Willy.

And it was.

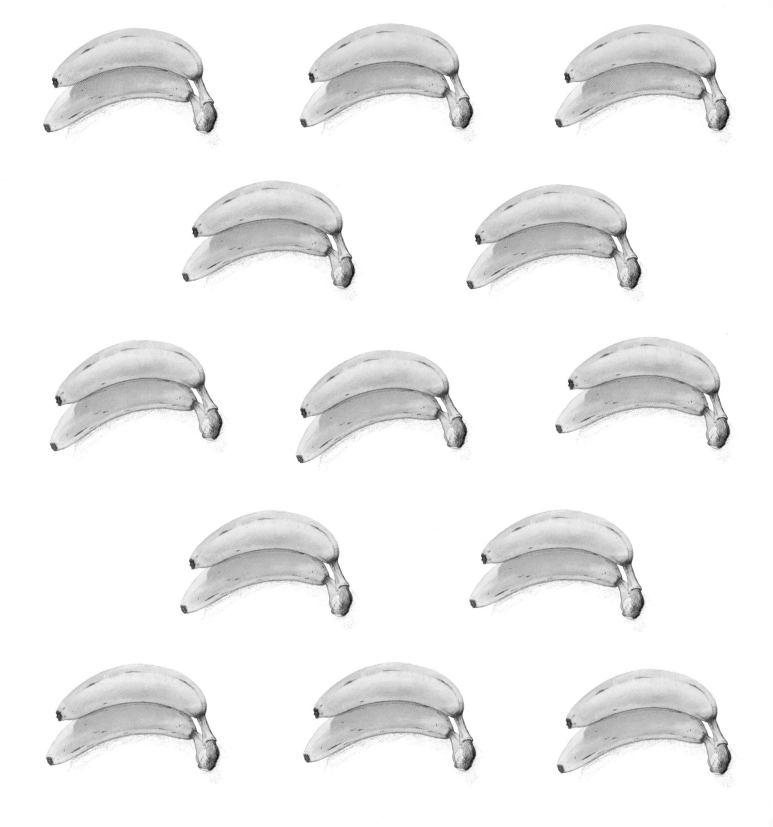